Sonic & Boom

Taking the Mystery out of the Detective Business

Sonic & Boom

Taking the Mystery out of the Detective Business

Robert C. Jones

A publication of

Eber & Wein Publishing

Pennsylvania

Library of Congress
Cataloging in Publication Data

ISBN 978-1-60880-792-5

Proudly manufactured in the United States of America by

Eber & Wein Publishing
Pennsylvania

I dedicate this book to Janina Parrott Jacobs who was the inspiration for the Sonic character Janina Julian.

Also to my three grandchildren— Brandon, Joshua, and Justin—who enjoy a good read in any genre.

CONTENTS

PROLOGUE

We just hung our shingle on the door of this ramshackle office. We're still cleaning up the place from a previous tenant—a private eye dick who fled, leaving behind a smell of rancid barbecue sauce along with trays of half-eaten fast food. I suppose he scarfed this food while deliberating a case or just wasting time, dozing off, and belching his food down in the process.

We picked it up for a song—this 18 x 20 office with a view of the alley, another building next door blocking out any sun we could filter into the place.

The building itself is a hundred-year-old office structure—gargoyles guarding the front entrance, bricks and masonry cracking off, littering the lawn and filling up the side alleyway.

A saving grace was a mahogany rolltop desk with many cubbyholes into which, I'm sure, will be placed the many important papers and documents to be easily accessible. These would be pulled out at appropriate times, impressing the many clients we are sure to entertain professionally in the coming months and years—building up a client business sure to be the best in the area, bar none.

I have come to this business late in life after having a career as a teacher—a teacher of special youth.

Now, on a pension, with time on my hands and not wanting to play golf in more than one league—plus a trip a week to the driving range to work out the many kinks in my game—I have arrived here in this dingy room, starting from scratch, setting up a business I know little about. But I am still idealistic enough to use my research skills, my size-thirteen shoe to hoof around uncovering clues, pounding a beat, and solving client problems, no matter the nature.

Having an associate law degree, I know the law in these matters and have some acquaintance with local officials, other lawyers, judges, municipal workers, and social workers, having taught in the local school system for over forty years.

I have attended many soirées over the years with these bureaucrats—public officials and private citizens attending—spreading cheer and goodwill during the holidays and often spreading swill and garbage and rumor-mongering the rest of the year.

So this indeed may be a somewhat dirty business. But I'm too young to sit, rock, and rot while my mind turns to jelly, my body bloating like some overinflated gas bag.

This brings me to my partner. She agreed, under perhaps some duress, to try this on a part-time basis over a thirty-day period.

We've known each other since kindergarten when she would invite me to her home for lunch. Back then, we walked home for lunch, then back to school. Kindergarten was in session all day.

I loved her mom's tomato soup, cheese sandwich, and milk—chocolate. But back then, I was more interested in her father's train set—the whole basement of Lionel trains, Plasticville buildings and homes, and little people positioned around the town.

In school, I was paired up with her to recite nursery rhymes on a homemade stage built by the teacher.

Our teacher would say we had the best voices for play-acting.

Through the grades, we occasionally talked to each other— nothing serious. My partner went on to be a musician—keyboard, songstress, classical pianist.

I tried my patience taking violin lessons in the sixth grade. I played "Reuben, Reuben"—A-E-D-G, some chords.

The boys laughed, and my partner shed a tear, I'm sure. It was back to sports for me, although I was in the middle and high school choir for a while.

3

Oh, here is a group photo of our sixth-grade class. My partner—top row, second from the right. My picture—second row down from the top, fourth from the right—the dude with the striped shirt. Then, although we worked in the same town—a small, insulated community—we never really made contact until about a year ago at one of those holiday soirées.

I'm sure she approached me first. Her intent seemed to be to wipe some spilled shrimp sauce off the shoulder of my white shirt.

"Don't we know each other?" Again, her line.

"I do believe we go back to elementary school," I responded, my attempt to be somewhat formal.

"I know you're a teacher—been here a long time, right?" Again, her lead.

"Yes, recently retired," my verbose follow-up.

We established the fact that I've never been married, and her husband had succumbed to cancer several years earlier.

That would have been that—my shirt having been cleaned—goodbye, Charlie Brown—but for one comment, which touched us both.

"I actually felt sorry for you when you played the violin. 'Reuben, Reuben,' wasn't it? But then I thought how nice—a fellow classmate, a boy, a male of the species who had the guts to stand in front of the class to play that piece while your boy playmates—giggling, heck, laughing out loud—made fun of your effort."

And that is how we connected. Fast forward to now, this moment, we're opening our new business with a sign on the door.

And oh yes, both of us will alternate sitting and attending to business at that mahogany rolltop desk. Share and share alike.

Her thirty-day trial was about to begin. She was the one who had the real law degree.

She claimed she could squeeze in this "gig" around all her other activities—music director at an area church, businesswoman balancing many business ventures, and now here to practice law in this dingy room. Hardly any light from the windows—this place "was a mess," as she would say over and over again.

She only had two requests. One: keep the shrimp sauce off my shirt. And two: I would be the leg man, the hustler—gathering material, putting files together, checking leads, facing people who were not nice.

Okay, let's get this show on the road. My name—Bob James, or BJ (the old-fashioned acronym). My partner—Janina Julian, or JJ (a not-so-old-fashioned acronym). We put together our namesakes. She being Sonic and me being Boom—Sonic-Boom. Now signed, sealed, and delivered—hoping to take the mystery out of the detective business.

DAY 1 — 8:00 AM

Janina grimaced. "You know this new business venture is just a scheme for you to get out of the house—or your apartment. I'll give it thirty days, then dump it; go back to my real life. What was I thinking?"

"That you like adventure, new toys, a chance to really crack a case, get your hands dirty—a little shrimp sauce on your blouse," Bob cut in.

"I see you've gone high-tech—Apple's latest, a pocket tape recorder, night binoculars, a smartphone. What is that piece of metal?" JJ asked, pointing to an object on the desk.

"Brass knuckles. Never know when I'll be in a back alley duking it out with some scab criminal."

"Oh, come now. You've got to be kidding. Give me a break; this isn't *Starsky and Hutch*."

"We've got to be prepared for any contingency. Who knows who might walk through that door at any minute, giving us maybe a murder case to solve with bad people involved, gunslingers just waiting to pounce on our detective carcasses," Bob responded excitedly.

"Speaking of guns," JJ asked matter-of-factly, "are you licensed to pack heat, and if so, are you willing to do so?"

"Glad you asked," Bob perked up. "I've got a Glock 17, 9MM pistol—accurate up to fifty feet—and a concealed weapon permit. I'm up to date on range time. All permits up to date."

JJ, getting up to leave, surveyed the dank, dark room. "Needs some curtains, a woman's touch. No knickknacks, just some final points—maybe a sofa, a recliner for all the business we'll be getting. I'll work on it."

"I'm a minimalist. Keep it simple, yet elegant."

"So, Mr. Sam Spade, we're in business—at least for the next thirty days. Keep me posted. I'll let you know when I'm comin' in. If you put a case together, need the bar, I'll be here. Don't expect me to be your sidekick, your dating companion, or your *call-me-anytime-just-to-talk* floozy. All business. *Capisce?*"

Bob, taken off guard, said, "Oh, I understand. There may be times we'll have to meet at a residence, a place of interest, a crime scene . . . "

JJ cut him off. "Just make sure when I'm contacted, it's about business. And I'll bill you by the hour. Hope you have the correct change and don't have to dip into your pension too deeply. See ya."

As JJ turned to leave, Bob's head spun a little. He noticed JJ's firm jawline, broad shoulders, tall athletic build, and cat-like movement as she pounced toward the door.

He remembered in the sixth grade—she had an all-knowing smile, as if to say, *Get on with your comment—I've got other things to do.* Not mean, but saucy and earthy—words that stuck with Bob: *saucy* and *earthy.*

His last thought before she exited: *We really are partners. This is what I've wanted since the sixth grade.* But now—*what did I get myself into? What in the name of Erle Stanley Gardner do I do now?* The butterflies settled slightly, but the gastric juices still churned. *Be businesslike . . . all business, big guy.*

He waited for the superintendent of the building to come and work on the thermostat.

He was going to test the toilet, flushing it properly—hoping no problems there.

He had brought clothes from home to hang in a small closet at the back of the room.

He jotted down other concerns for the super to look at.

Day one—complete. The ads would go out online and in a local newspaper. He also counted on word-of-mouth advertising.

He would be in court the next morning as a friend of the court. Some friends for that. He would write some more human-interest stories for a local gossip magazine—some money for that effort. Then his savings and pension would be dipped into for this tiny cubbyhole and all its utilities.

Go home. Get some sleep. Monday morning—a new venture will be here soon enough.

DAY 2 — 8:00 AM

Bob slipped on the envelope upon entering the office. *Take it to the desk. Come on, fool, open it up.*

"I'm in trouble – Save me – 3214 Park Ave. Lansing."

Now I have a cubbyhole to put this letter in—many cubby-holes, Bob thought.

So, I surmise I have a case. Or a prank. Emotions up and down. No phone number. No other information. JJ will be here soon from her court hearings, but why should I count on her acumen?

There's a word—acumen. The microwave has to be set up, as well as the food blender. Ugh. Green slime for breakfast—never.

How did time pass so quickly? There was a slight knock on the door.

"Do I have to announce my entry? You have a busted lock. Get it fixed," said JJ, now moving aggressively to the center of the room and revealing impatience.

"I've got some news. This letter came today—I'm in trouble. Save me—with an address," Bob blurted out.

JJ, looking around the shabby office, said, "So, I see you hooked up a microwave, hotplate, and a small TV. Do you plan on living here?"

Bob countered, "You're not listening to me. Case number one. A letter, an address. What's up with that?"

"Get real. Show me a court case. Something I can get my meaty hands on. Gotta go. Just checking your pathetic business. Where do I sign to be paid my retainer? You do have me on re-tainer, don't you?" With that, JJ stepped gingerly and made a beeline for the door, hurrying out and leaving the door more than ajar.

That's JJ—pushing ahead, wanting results, sometimes putting the cart before the horse. Being patient is not one of her salient traits. Say, there's another fancy word to add to my vocabulary; Merriam-Webster would be proud.

The phone people will be in tomorrow. He was sure the answering machine would soon fill up with job opportunities.

The letter was filed and locked up. Bob had a court date the following morning—a friend of the court hearing about a nonpayment of alimony case. Then he would head to the office, make some calls, try to rustle up some business and get a drive-through meal at a local taco restaurant tonight.

DAY 3

The coffee machine is working. *I should program it so it is freshly brewed when I enter at 8:00 AM*, Bob thought, making a mental note to do this. Arabica beans, dark-roasted, the water filtered through a Brita purifier—nothing too good for an aging, single male stuck in a sixties time warp, putting all his eggs in one basket . . . the final shootout at the OK Corral.

This morning, unshaven and in khaki mode, Bob almost tripped over the letter in a brown envelope.

Okay, what gives? he said to himself. *Read it, Mr. Ace Detective*:

> I'm being held prisoner. I've snuck out a few times, but he knows my where-abouts. What more do you need? You're not too far from our apartment. What are you waiting for?
>
> > Signed,
> > Desperate

He knew he could be walking into a trap. But then what if this person *is* in a desperate strait? Maybe wife abuse.

Okay, case number one, Bob thought excitedly. *I'll go to the address, pack my heat, and get to the bottom of this.*

"We got a situation here," Bob wrote in the logbook. He wasn't expecting JJ today but thought he should let her know where he is in case she comes in.

I need to confront this situation, even though it's probably a prank, he thought.

Bob pulled his favorite hat off the hat rack—a wide-brimmed Levine—and put on his Palo spring jacket. After checking himself in the mirror—looks being important in this business—he wedged his Glock into his tight-fitting Chinos.

The address on Park Avenue was right behind the state capital, an apartment number in a dingy old part of town. The urban renewal projects never got around to this particular area of the city.

Back in the day, Bob cavorted with many a politician who could "give a rat's patoot" about this part of the city, even though its presence was just beyond the shiny dome of the capital.

After going down two back alleys, he came to an apartment complex—he surmised twenty-four units.

Knocking on the door proved fruitless until it creaked open. This unit appeared to be a single room—kitchen, dinette, small living room—with a possible view of the back alley.

The blow to the back of the skull pummeled Bob into a state of total unconsciousness—perhaps a fatal blow.

"He's coming to. Bob, can you hear me?"

The buzzing sound in his ear didn't cease. His head throbbed, and his stomach churned. All that came out of his mouth was, "What the—what the…?"

"It's Janina. And I brought a local police officer. I followed the address in your daily log. Just stopped by the office to bring you some color swatches for the drapes I said I'd spring for. Couldn't find you there, but I knew you had office hours today.

"Now I find your carcass on a floor in this dink of a hellhole. Don't you know to take more precautions? This is no prank, dear boy," Janina said, shaking her head.

"What gives? Trouble on the dating front—jealous lover from long ago? Luring your butt to no-no land, you—"

"Just get me a wet cloth," said Bob, starting to sit up. "I don't feel any blood. Thanks for trailing me. Didn't I say we were a team? I don't know anything about that note or what this address means—never been to this part of the city. I've settled all my old scores—at least, I think I have.

"Damn head. Back to the office. First, I'll case the joint. Like that expression." Bob's voice trailed off to a whimper, his head throbbing even worse now.

Back in the office, Bob and Janina were again at odds. Janina spoke with disdain:

"So, my fine-feathered friend, what were you thinking? Don't respond. You don't know the difference between literal and metaphorical.

"So, here are the swatches for the drapes. But this place needs more than just a woman's touch.

"Okay, Mr. Detective Man, you've now got twenty-six days to make this a go. I've got other places to go. I'm not wasting anymore of my time with you today. Oh, and you'll get my bill to bail your behind out of your sloppy detective work."

Bob's head still burned, his demeanor in a defeatist mode. He gazed at Janina, maybe hoping for some sympathy. But no, she sighed in relief and said over her shoulder as she exited, "Call me when a real case comes in. Wait until you see my bill for my stress—twenty-six days, old man!"

It was past quitting time, but Bob couldn't pay himself for overtime. He looked at the swatches.

"Well, the reddish-orange shade will go well with the wallpaper. I'll choose this swatch. So she really wants to turn this room into a livable space. We really are partners," he said to himself.

Bob set the coffee machine to begin brewing at 7:45 AM for the next day. He told himself he was getting cozy in this space.

His head still throbbed. *A good night's sleep is all I need,* he told himself. He needed a mystery to solve, though, some challenge to make Janina more a part of the team.

This misstep was just a minor setback.

DAY 4

The call came at precisely 2:00 PM. A muffled voice said: "There's trouble comin' to this town. The big boys are taking a sack full of change outta the vault. I'm just a whistleblower. My life doesn't mean peanuts. I know you by reputation. A stand-up guy. This new business of yours—just gettin' off the ground. I want to retain your services. I'll send a fee to your bank account. I already hacked it. Look, tomorrow, you'll notice a big difference in the account. I'll call tomorrow sometime and provide you with more details."

The muffled voice became unrecognizable—then the line went dead.

How did he hack into my bank account? A cybercrime, to be sure. So now I'm putting my financial life at risk. I'll check my account in the morning since I don't do banking on my smartphone.

I'm beginning to think that, in my world, I'm just some antiquated dinosaur—not aware of my tech surroundings nor what this new world of human relations is all about.

Bob locked up—or so he thought.

JJ was right. Examining the lock, Bob concluded the damn thing was indeed busted. He would call the super in the morning.

Thieves can steal my Apple computer—that's about the only thing of value here, he thought.

Bob spent another night on the couch. His apartment was a mess, not having been cleaned in a couple of weeks.

At least I've had a change of underwear each day. What did Mom say? 'If you have a heart attack or are taken to the hospital for some reason, have clean underwear on.'

DAY 5

Bob was late for work, as he stopped off at his bank and found that a hefty sum of $25,000 had been added to his account.

What he would have to do for this amount, he could only imagine.

No one broke into the office overnight. The coffee machine was heated up by the time he arrived, and he popped a sausage biscuit into the microwave.

The answering machine showed he had two messages asking to purchase medical insurance.

He thought JJ might stop by. Maybe even bring some curtains to hang. *It would be her way*, he thought, *to show me a sample but not trust my judgment and just buy the curtains outright and, of course, present me with the bill. I'll bet she already has a bill for me to pay just for her showing up these past few days.*

These thoughts and others make the time pass more quickly. At 2:00 PM, the phone rings.

This time, the voice was less muffled, and the message came across loud and clear:

"Listen to me good, Mr. Detective. So, you checked your account this morning. Surprise, surprise. I will ask you to break into our state's capital and make your way to the top floor, where you'll go to a utility storage room marked JANITORS SUPPLY CLOSET. Go in and pull down the front of the paper towel machine. You will find a computer stick with all the information you need to start your investigation. I'll give you three days to complete this task; then, we'll talk again. Formulate a plan of attack because, my Sherlock friend, this is war. In the meantime, keep your thoughts to yourself. There will be dire consequences if you spill these beans. The preservation of our state's democracy is at stake. Remember, you're taking the chances. If caught, your ass is on the chopping block. If and when you are successful, we'll talk again. I'll know if you succeeded. We have our compatriots working on our side. You are but a third party. You're taking all the chances now. If we can trust you further, perhaps you can help our cause. If not, you, as the saying goes, will be "dead in the water."

With that last comment, the phone went dead.

Bob's stomach churned. His head ached. This again was a prank or some conspiratorial nutcase spewing anti-government invectives or perhaps—*no, can't be*—a real attempt by some group to take over the state's government—maybe even by force.

I didn't sign up for this heavy-duty activity. Maybe these are just pranksters, but the large amount in my checking account is real, with more to come if I just follow instructions.

Then again, should I tell JJ? She's gotta know what I'm doin' bein' my partner and all.

She's coming in tomorrow. I'll be concise. Act as if I know what I'm doing. How much she'll buy into it, I don't know. She just wants the court assignments. Well, tough luck. She's going to have to suck it up. We'll work together.

With that self-thought processed through his mental system, he left the small office and went home. For dinner, he opened a can of spaghetti and meatballs and crashed on the couch, where he slept for nine hours. He woke up refreshed and ready to tackle another day. He would confront JJ and start the detective ball rolling.

Who am I kidding? His stomach was churning out of control, and he experienced night sweats frequently. His constipation over these last three days was eating him alive.

DAY 6

When Bob arrived at his office the next morning, he was surprised to find his lock fixed and his coffee brewing, the smell of Arabica beans permeating the place, drowning out the previous tenant's smell of dried-up fast food, rancid body odors, and an aftershave smell even a gigolo wouldn't wear.

Preparation H didn't do the trick the previous evening. He now felt bloated, a stuffed, cramped feeling. Maybe a Fleet enema would do the trick.

JJ bolted through the door. "Just seeing the light of day in here. Did you select a swatch?"

Bob countered, "Look, I've news . . . a client . . . hear me out . . . someone, something . . . wants me—you and me—to find a computer program at the state capital." Now out of breath, Bob continues, "Bring it back here . . . a big scandal brewing . . . a breaking case . . . a muffled voice on the phone saying they put money in my account," Bob finished, now completely out of breath.

"Okay, okay, slow down, grand master. I'm just punchin' your daily time clock. Nothin' doin'. I'm goin'—bye-bye now." JJ headed for the door.

"Wait, have a seat. Let me explain," Bob pleaded earnestly, reaching out and taking JJ by the wrist, urging her to sit down.

Startled, JJ complied.

"So, some guy called yesterday and wanted me to take his case. He claimed the state's government was being hijacked—I don't know what that means—and paid me money in my account. Good to go.

"We—I—need to procure a computer stick in the state capital, bring it back, and see what's on it. Then I have to wait for this dude's directions at 2:00 PM sharp the day after we get the chip. Then we go from there. May be some high officials in our state's government doin' some mischief.

"I've got the directions," said Bob, now calming down a bit.

JJ reiterated: "So, I suppose you want me to tag along to the capital, get this chip stick, bring it back, look at it, discern what it means, wait for a call from Mr. Anonymous, and go from there."

"You summarize well. I said you'd be paid. More money coming if and when we follow Mr. A's directions," Bob said, thinking JJ would buy into the plan.

JJ again sums things up through a nonsensical discussion. "But you're the leg man, the guy who puts together a case, the—"

Bob interrupts: "I need you as a lookout. I can get into the back stairs, make the climb to the janitor's closet, and find the stick. I need assurance—a distraction at the bottom of the stairs. In other words, a lookout to make sure no one's climbing those stairs. I'll wear a janitor's uniform under my regular clothes. We'll get through security okay, but we must avoid the cameras. As a legislative aid back in the day, I know every nook and cranny in that place, including the janitor's closet up those flight of back stairs."

JJ concluded again with her own summation: "So, I'm your lookout. Let me get this straight. You better have money for this effort. So, we get this computer chip, bring it back to this place and wait for Mr. Anonymous to contact us. All the while, someone out there is watching our every move. And if the capital police stop us, search us, suspect us, hold us for questioning, throw us in the hoosegow, we just eat crow, make bail, and have a record. Me, the pristine can't-do-anything-wrong lawyer, thirty clean years of truth, justice, and the American way—eat it all on one breaking and entering, the state capital no less, no law practice ever again, no great parties, reputation soiled beyond recognition. All for your new uppity detective business. You still have strawberry jelly on your soiled winter hunters shirt. Okay, I'm in."

JJ fired these lines rapidly, Bob not having a chance to breathe, only echoed: "So we have tomorrow to make this happen. And this is only the first step. The following day, Mr. Anonymous will call at 2:00 PM to give us directions as to our next move.

"We'll meet tomorrow at 8:00 AM, coffee ready. I'll have a breakfast biscuit. Do you want one, JJ?"

"Leave me out of your fast food indulgences. I'll be here at 8:00. So now my bill is really running up a tab.

"I'll be your lookout. I'd better be able to keep this excursion separate from my regular job. You get me any deeper into your dark world you'll be more than sorry." With those comments, JJ again stormed toward the door and uttered, "Lock fixed—good sign. 8 AM it is."

Bob was left to program the coffee for the next morning. His only thought to himself—*and to think I had the color to the drapes all figured out. She didn't even give me a chance to tell her.*

DAY 7

"So here we are. Made it through the metal detector. Position yourself at the bottom of the stairs over there. I know the back way to the bathroom marked JANITOR'S CLOSET," said Bob, giving JJ directions even as she had what he interpreted as a scowl on her face.

"Be my lookout. Phones on." He climbed the stairs in his work clothes, the same as the capital crew. The first door confronted. Locked. Get your card out, slide it up and down, and wait for the click. No click. Grab the knob. Pull. No luck. No other way to enter.

Now what? I'm stuck on the first level. Maybe there's a regular way to get to the sixth level—the Janitor's Closet. Think, man, think. Go back down. Find the inside passageway. But you may run into a worker who doesn't know who you are. Okay, I'm wearing a fake badge. Talk to Janina. Hatch another plan. There are, he told himself, *those front stairs. I've been there before. The upper chambers, it was called, were above the gallery level. Let's go with this plan. We can still make it. Now, don't be too obvious. Janina is still a lookout. Let her be discreet. Wander slowly around the lobby. Nothing, really, for her to do.*

He opened the door to the main floor and was almost nose-to-nose with Janina. "That didn't take long. Good job, number one detective. Let me see this famous chip."

"I don't have it. We'll have to find another way. Let's go through the lobby. There's a front entrance to the stairway," said Bob, out of breath, thinking he could evade the embarrassment of not getting the prize and formulate a new plan in the same instant.

Maybe JJ would be too overwhelmed by my mixed messages and would just follow me out onto the main lobby of the building now that I'm taking the unusual position of a leadership role in this, she would surmise, to be a flimsy excuse for a legitimate detective-like caper.

She mumbled under her breath, "Let an amateur at work—get amateur results."

Before Bob took five steps onto the rotunda floor, JJ was gone. Five minutes went by—no JJ.

Maybe she left. Could I blame her? Doubts as to what in the name of Columbo was he doing here amidst all this legislative scandalizing—the good, the bad, and the ugly hanging out their laundry, dirty and otherwise.

He had spent many hours here back in the day as a legislative aide before his teaching days—young and idealistic! Change the world—right the many wrongs.

He never went in for that hippy business. It was always nose to the grindstone; yes sir, no sir.

He even got a chance to summarize some of the legislation, writing briefs for his house of representative mentor.

Then, there were the press briefings he was to write. Smooth things over. He was good at that. He didn't even have to use a thesaurus. He was young and knew what his generation wanted. He was, he knew, helping the older, stodgy, three-piece suitors, who were bought out by the insurance, pharmaceutical, and trucking industries who gave tons of money for these "crown jewel pissant ne'er-do-wells" to vote their way.

He became disillusioned and went into teaching. More idealism. More disenchantment. But he stuck it out.

Now, there is some inane scheme by who knows what and on whom. Overthrow the system. What was the system anymore anyway?

"Is this what you're looking for?" JJ opened her palm, revealing a computer stick possibly charged with information that would rock this assembly to its virtual knees, or so Bob thought, referring to his lifelong dreamy, ethereal frame of reference, his mind always the idealizing, seeming to lack, at times, that old-fashioned, down-to-earth stable doubting Thomas realistic state of mind.

"Yes," he said, his face now red. "But . . . but, how?"

"Don't ask." JJ, a bit edgy, yet still her matter-of-fact self, said, "Let's get this back to the office and see what's on it. Tomorrow, wait for the 2 PM call. Further instructions forthcoming."

In the office, JJ slotted the stick. Both waited for the computer to warm up and then viewed the picture on the screen.

At first, they heard some mumbling. Then, around a table, four figures came into view.

The whole video was still somewhat of a blur and seemed to be taken from a few tables away. Then, it came more into focus.

Bob gasped as he recognized the faces—four of the most influential senators in the state. Their tone was somber.

"Take away the state's freedom clauses—much like what's in the federal constitution—and we'll have our usurping power. Our state's constitution as one item would give our senate the power to override that clause."

"Yes," the second senator spoke up: "The emergency power clause, which states the senate and house may take control of all affairs of state if and when the voters deem necessary—the state constitution could be suspended due to the treachery and precarious condition of the current state of affairs."

"Sounds like a lot of gobbledegook to me. A lawyer's handprint all over that piece of legislation."

The third senator spoke up: "But listen, fellas. This may be our chance to grab the brass ring. Think of the power we'd have. All the contracts with our special interest boys. The power of the purse."

The fourth senator, the quietest and maybe most practical in the group, spoke up: "Okay, fellas, and how do you propose to put this vote before the people of this state? Pull the wool over the eyes of the citizenry. So we have more power. How do we use this power—er authority—and to what end? We'd also need to control the national guard—get that group under our control. With the national guard and state police under our control, we can go after the twenty or so right-wing so-called patriot organizations. The citizens would thank us for that clean-cut service. It might be a bloodbath for a while, but we will do more than that simple deed.

"We'd wreak havoc on the whole governmental process. Think, boys, we who are at this table can puncture holes in the right-wingers and can destroy the elitist left-wingers. Those boys; one lady senator; those online rich money grabbers—grifters, I say, who want to send us into bankruptcy, demanding mandates the average schmuck on the street can't meet. Higher energy bills—these are solar panel freakouts. E.V. pumping pissants. A little Shakespeare there. A little discomfort they repute, long-term clean energy, electric vehicles, and windmills in my backyard. They are getting rich on the government dole. Research grants here, kickbacks from the energy freaks there."

The third senator spoke again: "Lordy, Lordy. We're grab-bin' the feats hard and fast. The rich elitists and the conservative patriot end-of-the-world crowd. And don't forget we can grab ass and put pressure on the pharmaceutical industry in our state, which is pushing pills on the weak unsuspecting public. Crackdown on doctors dispensing unnecessary medications on our unsuspecting naïve citizenry."

The second senator summarized the meeting. "So, gentle-men, do-gooders that we are, I know we can use this emergency powers clause for the good of the people. I deal with these federal lobbyists all the time, weaseling their way into the state's business. It'll only take a vote of our committee to put our plans into effect. Attach it to the Omnibus crime bill. Guncheck. Lockup firearms.

Felony for letting youngsters get to their family's firearms. No one will complain. Pure and simple.

"We then swoop in. Take charge. Bill is up for a vote in two weeks. Thirty days after that, the law takes effect. Plenty of lame duck ne'er-do-wells votin' yes on these crime bills. Never readin' 'em."

The fourth senator summarized the already summarized meeting. "Ah yes, steak tartare. Good place to meet gentlemen. Now, lay low. You know Cedric, the do-gooder, the senate chamber master, will move this bill to the front of the line. Push the yes button, fellow senators. *Whoosh*—the sound of victory. Marshall our forces then move swiftly. By the end of the fiscal year, our power will be complete. Off and running.

"We'll meet next week at a different restaurant. Draw up plans. Decide on the first point of attack."

"The patriot groups have to go first," the third senator lamented.

"Not so fast. Don't be hasty. This meeting is adjourned," stated the fourth senator, pounding his fist on the table.

The film became blurry. The audio deadened. Bob plucked the stick from the slot. "So, where are we? We wait for further instructions here in the office 2:00 PM tomorrow.

"Do you think there is any credence to their ideas? Or just a group of old-school politicians with one last fling on their pie-in-the-sky fantasy world? Through committee, onto the floor for a vote."

"No house vote is needed on this one. No need to pass it by their ways and means committee. No money involved, gentlemen."

The picture faded. The sound garbled. Then darkness.

"I know each of those boys. Two very well. Good folk. All four old-timers who do things the old-fashioned way. Work across the aisle to get a good bill passed. Can't imagine they'd be pullin' stunts to grab power for power's sake.

"They must have thought this thing through and through. At their age, there is no need to do something very risky to jeopardize their pension. I think they all have grandkids. Good family values . . . " Bob trailed off, now at a loss for words.

Janina's demeanor changed from bewilderment at first to concern, her brows furrowed at this serious business.

"Okay, some thoughts here: I want to know who this whistle-blower is. He may just be whistling in the wind. Those four senate boys just passin' gas—no real credence to whatever they are professin'."

"So we wait till the morrow at 2 PM and listen to what the whistleblower has to say."

Janina interrupted: "So I'm involved. You say this whistle-blower has already dumped coins into your vault? I want fifty percent. Half and half. I've got too many other obligations to hang my hat on just your door and your reputation."

"Okay, I'll be here tomorrow shortly before 2 PM. Can we call this a caper yet?"

"Just sounds like old cronies blowin' off senior steam. They can't wait to dig into their pension. All those luscious retirement benefits."

Janina came close to Bob. "So, you think you know these moldy oldies? Older than you, but not by much. You know this world is mucked up. Not the people's business. Just a bunch of cronies living on everyone else's dime. We all know the chant. Nothin' changes, dear boy. Everyone has a price. Even you, señor.

"So I'll be here—one time. Your bill runnin' a fever. At any rate, you've chosen a color for the drapes. I see the swatches on that table. But did you just say eeny, meeny, miney, mo? Good choice, though. I'll give ya some credit.

"Oh, and by the way, my choice of wine is Chateau Pichon Longueville—Virginia de La Contessa. Have it ready ASAP." Janina left unannounced coming and going.

Bob now looked forward to another gut-wrenching, stomach-churning night. Then, he would be back in this office the following day when he would receive a 2 PM call from the whistleblower.

The two most important items—he knew Janina's choice of wine, and he apparently picked an acceptable color for the drapes. Progress, to be sure. Oh, and the lock to the outer door was fixed.

DAY 8

At 1:00 PM, Bob unlocked the door to his office and smelled the coffee brewing. The timer worked. He even sanitized the office bathroom. He opened the shades, and the view of the brick building next door reminded him of the cheap office space he was paying rent on.

He was accumulating a library of law books, self-help books, and a couple of nutrition books he picked up at local flea markets.

His diet, however, still consisted of chef whomever that came with a can opener.

He knew Janina wanted to be paid today, so he yanked a check from his checkbook. He knew it wouldn't bounce. Better not.

Would this Mr. Whistleblower add some more greenbacks into his account? He felt an eerie sense of being violated as he knew this whistleblower was hacking into his bank account, putting money in to be sure, but could just as easily drain his account.

A knock at the door made him jump. Janina appeared looking as if she was dressed for a grand affair. *Was that a tweed jacket? Pantsuit. Buckled boots. Two Egyptian scarves slung around her neck in opposite directions. Christian Dior all the way. No, Prada. But what do I know? My fashion sense is limited to jeans, support hose, bunion support, and Sketchers shoes. The last gout episode was a real bitch.*

"So, knock me over," Bob commented.

"So, why don't I have a chair to these proceedings? Almost 2 PM—your show, Sherlock."

Bob moved a chair closer to Janina. "So, do you like the

drapes? Your color and design. Although it faces a brick court-yard. Not a nice view."

The phone rang twice. Bob picked it up. "So now you see and hear the problem. You were chosen as our contact because you are a has-been. I know nothing. Shadows from the past.

"So now we—yes, a group of us—want to put your sorry ass in harm's way for a price. Infiltrate. Go to 233 Marshall Street to-morrow. Get your packet of information. Nevermind what we are all about. The cleanup process is just beginning.

"My muffled voice on your tracker will never be traced. So piss off. Another sum to be placed in your bank account. Proceed, you back-in-the-day piece of shrapnel crap." The phone went dead.

Janina only laughed. "Sounds like a junior high prank! May-be middle school. So report to your money-laundering friend. My bill keeps getting bigger and bigger."

She took a slip of paper from her blouse and handed it to Bob.

"Here is your check." He gave Janina a check from his lapel pocket.

"Not enough for this caper. Just your down payment. Get wise, Bob—or should I call you Roberto? Go to that address to-morrow. There will be further instructions, I'm sure.

"Better do a bio on those videoed. It seems they really do want to clean up this state's corrupt, sleazy government. Good luck. Seems you are in the middle of a real dilemma."

Bob responded: "Can I at least inform you as to the back-ground of these four senators? I know them well. Give me a chance to elaborate."

Janina shot back, "So tell me, what in the name of the peo-ple's republic of our great state is goin' on? It isn't as if I need the greenbacks. I'm only intrigued. These four senators—are they your piss-off friends from the days of yore?"

"Just hear me out," Bob said, seeing as Janina was agitated and ready to leave. She sat down, the chair not to her liking.

"I heard Michael Holiday. He's called the Boy Wonder of our state's politics—his career marred by personal tragedy. Wife died at age forty. One son died of an opioid overdose. Career came to a halt decades ago. Last year now in politics."

"Oh boy. Intellectual Joe Frantove. Petosky whiz kid. Another super street-smart politician. Wrote many briefs for him back in the day. Put his heart and soul into cleaning up the mess in government.

"No ethics in this state. Kickbacks galore. Old Joe worked for years tryin' to put some sort of reform in place to no avail. Poor sap. Divorced. Wife ran off with a gigolo from South America. Rio, I believe, some bureaucrat from a rebel party there. She just fell off the grid.

"Then Leonard Babcock. Dealt with all the lobbyists over the years. Many skeletons in his closet. Maybe a billionaire. Kickbacks. Slush fund money. The old way of doin' business. Maybe tired of the grind. Salted away enough stash to put the grandkids and great-grandkids through their college years and beyond. Nice guy, but don't turn your back on him.

"Then last and maybe least, the new kid on the block, Senator Caleb Clark. The I'm-cleaning-up-the-yard-on-my-watch big chief who moves fast—a cut-the-crap politician. No holds barred.

"Young as he is—he's the godson, not godfather, of state politics—he'll mow anyone in his way into rotten mulch. So he runs with the senior crowd."

Janina, hanging on to the doorknob, sent out a wisecrack. "Sounds as if you got 'em pegged. Okay, let me know what's goin' on, Roberto. You move on with your life, I with mine. Got some court dates comin' up—no time for your shenanigans. Thanks for the bread. Your bill keeps growin'."

"Remember, you do the footwork. I'm the brains. You're goin' into the deep state. I'll ride your coattails. Get reimbursed."

As she started through the door, Bob chimed, "So, Janina, how did you procure that stick?"

Was that a demure smile or just a smirk on her face?

"Yours to find out, dear boy."

One last gasp comment, "Prada."

"Get it right, Roberto. Balenciaga. Suspended halter cotton twill. Your paltry pension wouldn't even cover the two buttons on the sleeve."

The door slammed shut.

DAY 9

Bob found the address. This time, no funny business. Get whatever directions this whistleblower had; do whatever, within reason, not getting in harm's way. He wondered what the end game was.

He had his Glock 17, 9 MM pistol strapped on with the hope he wouldn't have to use it.

This neighborhood was in his old stomping ground, where new homes were abandoned. No more boys' training school down the block. The 119th Armory base closed many years previous.

The side entrance is best. Front door ramshackled, barred from entering. Two knocks. No reply. Covered with wooden crates. Three knocks. A stirring. Two hooded bodyguards jerked the door open.

"Blindfold on, sir."

"What the . . . "

A hammerlock. Blindfold attached. He was shoved down a hallway. A right turn. Pushed down on a chair. A long silence. The guards stood one on each side.

"Welcome to our humble abode," said a muffled voice, barely recognizable. "I'll do the talking. You do the listening. Then, the walking. Billions of dollars are at stake here.

"You've been chosen by our group to infiltrate our esteemed legislature. You have somewhat of a sordid past but a decent enough reputation. You're to be one of the freshman senator's aides. The senator was a real loud, rambunctious youth, a sell-out to any factor. Help him. Research the legislation to be brought up for a vote. Introduce him to your cronies still left. Snoop around. If you have any important information, buzz us back. Here are our computer codes, platform, and email address. We're very secure, though; we sometimes delve into the deep dark state.

"Our mission is to defend freedom at any cost, good guys that we are. You already know the four senators ready to turn the system upside down. Are we a part of that rat pack? No need for you to know at this moment. Another payment just made it to your bank account. Billions of dollars at stake here. You'll be a part of history.

"Isn't it refreshing to know you have some credence left in our small political community? Sorry for the blindfold and the strong-arm tactics. Didn't know if you would cooperate or not. You must need a few more dollars to add to your puny teacher pension.

"All clear now? By the way, don't involve your alleged partner in crime. In the courtroom, she's known as Janina the Sassy Lassie. A by-the-book lawyer but a real pain in the patoot. *Capisce*?

"Leave the way you came in." Bob was handed a business-size envelope, then grabbed by each elbow and ushered out the side door, which slammed shut behind him.

His car was parked two blocks away—his idea of taking precautions. He would go back to his office to process this meeting.

How should he approach Janina? Tell her what this brut told him or tell her nothing. And really now, was there anything more for her to do? Maybe it was time for him to part ways. He was going undercover, and she stuck out like a sore thumb.

Sonic and Boom just may be on their last leg. And to think he was just beginning to get used to her brusque yet cultural ways. And he never knew there were so many shades of green and blue—tints she called them.

This office now felt cozy with both of them working together and making a go of it.

His last thoughts that evening. *Who were these thugs, hood-*

lums, ne'er do wells, public servants, ex-politicians, ex-cons, or whatever they pretended to be or to represent?

I know they're amateurs. They didn't put me down when I entered the house. Something strange about the big chief. I've heard the word credence used many times to an extreme by one of my colleagues back in the day. And a particular aftershave, a strong musky scent that a former politician used, permeats the room I'm in.

Who can get a stomach ache from a dish of ramen noodles? Maybe it was the Schenleys' scotch as a bedtime chaser. Gurd acting up again. The gout's beginning to pierce my big toe again. Then again, these pains may just be minor aches compared to having to face Janina in just a few hours—no sleep for the wicked.

DAY 10

Coffee on. Shades open. More books placed on a shelf. Lock fixed. Working. Out of jeans today. Coat and tie. In the PM meet freshman senator. Detail your background. Schmooze. Act friendly.

The informant transferred more cash into his account. Bob was still at a loss as to who these whistle-blowers were and who they represented—amateur sleuths at best.

You want action. You got action. But I'm just an observer at this point. You, with a questionable, ho-hum reputation. But reliable. Being used is not a problem.

The door banged open. "So, I see you have a comfortable chair for me to sit on."

For Bob, this was getting tiresome. Get this woman out of your life. "Yes, sit. Got some news. I'm now working on duty for a freshman senator. Yesterday, I met with the whistleblower. I was given instructions: Report suspicious behavior to a given address. I was given computer information, email, and other places to report suspicious behavior. I'm back in the saddle and keeping an eye on the Four Horsemen—this term coined by the legislative establishment.

"So, Janina, I don't know where you fit in anymore. You are called the Sassy Lassie by the court establishment. We exist in a small town, you know."

"Letting me go is not an option; we're tied at the hip. I've got news that's going to blow your mind. Just sit and listen."

"Can I at least offer you this morning's brew? A Honduran blend—a Juan Valdez special. He handpicked 'em himself," said Bob, trying to slow down what he perceived to be Janina's impetuous behavior. "Don't you now like the ambiance in our quaint little office? I've been paid again. The whistleblower's comin' through."

Janina sipped lightly from a mug Bob bought that said *Best Partner Ever.*

She moved her chair closer to him. "You're being set up—a pawn in a big scheme. Billions of dollars are at stake. Just you—collateral damage.

"Don't know if it's too late to back out. Probably not. People movin' behind the scenes gettin' the big show ready. My source is comin' through. That new state senator you'll be workin' with—not as naïve as you may think. He'll bring you in . . . very congenial. He'll want you to interview one of the patriot groups. You'll be killed. A mighty uproar ensues. Citizens frantic. You on the news—now a martyr.

"You're just shark bait for the cause. These four senators are tightening their grip. Emergency Powers Act legislation goes through. State of emergency declared. Warfare begins."

Janina moves closer to Bob. "And my sources are never wrong. You see, you are one of the good guys. Always wanting the right end result. A regular fellow.

"But you see, your whole life is predicated on the fact you believe in the sanctity and honesty of mankind—that basically the average Joe, by nature, is honest, upright, forthright, true to his beliefs, above board in all matters. Should I go on?

"Oh, I know you and many others like you. Regular Boy Scouts. Sorry to disappoint you, dude. You're out of your league. The big boys eat you for lunch and excrete you in the middle of the night during a bad bowel movement."

Bob blushed, turning angrily to Janina. "Cut the crap language. I'm being paid for my expertise. Yeah, okay, I'm a good guy or semi decent anyway. I've got a job to do here. Somebody actually values my experience and my input in these matters.

"These are perilous times, to be sure. I'm not retired yet. This job, assignment, duty—call it what you want—gives me renewed energy. I feel important again.

"So many of my friends are dead after retirement. On pensions. Getting by but no action. The cards they play at the senior center are not enough. Golf ceases to interest them enough. Something about the adrenaline rush, the chances we take later in life. One more job for the Gipper.

"For me, something about self-respect. I couldn't live with myself if I didn't move on this case. So, I'm naïve. Guilty, I suppose." Bob, out of breath, had more to say but just wheeled his chair around and stared out the window at the brick wall across the alley.

"So, you don't think I haven't gone through my own turbulent times? I've played many charades in my life. I'm not as cold-hearted as you think I am.

"I like being Sassy Lassie. I win in court. I also get behind the scenes. I know what's goin' on in the big bad business of politics. This state is the worst for ethics, and almost everyone is sellin' their souls for the almighty buck and not blinkin' an eyelash of remorse.

"Poor country bumpkins—the average citizens of this great state—are helpless, paying more and more taxes. The state is burning money into a hellhole and gettin' nothing in return.

"So do your due diligence before you go further down this rathole. Maybe now you, too, have sold your soul to the bad dude in the basement. You know, Bob, I picked you to come here. You didn't choose me. You had guts playin' that violin in front of our sixth-grade class, especially in front of those pre-pubescent males who showed their bully ways in your face."

"So, you actually care for me? *Like* me? And you'll actually pay for the drapes? Yeah, I'll do my due diligence all right. I'll proceed cautiously. Be back here tomorrow afternoon. You'll report then? Thanks for the support."

There was a moment of silence. Janina half smiled, searching for a summation courtroom style.

"Let's not play word games anymore. We're both big people with many holes and hurts in our psyche. See you tomorrow. And I'll pay for the drapes." She rose. Bob was fully aware of her stature—imposing, tall, her Haute couture clothes matching her confident demeanor.

She walked like a runway model to the door and turned around. "Okay, tomorrow. And by the way—no bill for today. A freebie."

DAY 11

The starched collar itched, and the blue tie was pulled too tight. Where did the extra weight come from? A definite gut protruding. Haven't had these digs on in a few years. Friday casual marked past days, even loosy goosy among the court crowd.

"Welcome, Bob. Let me introduce you to our fellow committee members. Got a stack of paperwork for ya.

"Senator George Munson, Sammy Trudell, Bill Swanson, meet Bob . . .

"All of 'em will be drinkin' buddies in no time. You go back a long way in this chamber and all. You come highly recommended. Good with paperwork. Let me know whom we can pressure on a bill, how we can load up a bill with perks, and how we can pork barrel a bill and sneak it through.

"Oh, you'll be called on for every vote. Work part-time. There will be some paperwork, which you can take to your office.

"By the way, our committee here investigates threats to our state's constitution—a special committee set up only a few months ago by Senator Holiday and his cronies. You're at the right place at the right time. Seems there's some threats to our well-being here at our state's capitol.

"By the way, next week at this time, you'll be goin' to a small community in the Thumb. You'll interview one of twenty-three patriot groups' leaders, one Highway Joe Smotherman—a real patriot, that one.

"Yeah, we'll give ya one of our best armed guards. Here's the list of questions to ask. Just collectin' information, that's all. He's agreed to put his story on record.

"Use our van. See my chauffeur next week for the keys. You're all set. There's no bills comin' to a vote but take these files with ya; I'm sure you know how to summarize 'em. You can drop 'em off at your convenience. If any emergency comes up, you'll be the first to know.

"Oh, yeah—you'll get paid—a bit more than other aides, you bein' more experienced by far.

"Nice meetin' ya, Bob."

Back at the office, Bob, who was good at reading expressions—raised eyebrows, throw-ya-to-the-wolves behavior, under the bus—didn't detect any errant behavior. Yet, this gig was seemingly too easy.

Sleep on it. Open up a can of something and have a few beers to relax. Dexter. *That was the series to watch. No, no,* Game of Thrones. *But then, who would I compare notes with anyway? And no football pool or water cooler talk to spice the time. Just Janina. What did she mean when she said, "I chose you"? Sleep on it. Fluff up your pillow, Señor. Drapes are paid for. A plus.*

DAY 12

The super actually turned the heat up in the building. The vents to this office became unclogged. Bob pulled the rolltop adjacent to the vents, and the heat began to warm his legs.

I actually have two friend-of-the-court cases coming up before my jaunt next week to meet Highway Joe. Good thing Senator Pankow is providing a bodyguard. Maybe the Highway Man is a good guy just doin' some maneuvers, biblical, like preparing for the endgame.

And last night's trip to Lucky Lou's Liquor Emporium produced the favored wine on Janina's palate, though it was costly.

Bob heard a knock on the door, and then it opened.

"Don't want to scare you." Janina's voice was quieter and more modulated than in previous visits. "Just checking in. Got to go out of town for a few days. How did it go with the senator?" Janina eased her way to a chair next to Bob. He quit trying to guess what her style sense and dress might be today.

"Fine, okay. Just rubbin' elbows. Drinkin' buddies to be and all. Movin' next week to interview the dude Highway Joe."

"I'm telling you, you're going into a trap. But hey, who am I to say don't go. What kind of flowers do you prefer for your funeral?"

Bob was now used to this ribbing, serious as it may be intended. "More funds were put into my account. Now, I have an obligation.

"Say, wait a minute. Can we put this jabbering on hold? Got a surprise for ya." He took the bottle of wine from the cooler and showed the label to Janina.

"You've got great taste. You picked a good year, too. But save it for a real special occasion. Not even New Year's Eve or our birthdays—I mean a *real* occasion.

"Anything else today I should know about?" Janina caught a glimpse of the new drapes, and a slight smile lit up half her face.

"It seems warmer in here. I mean temperature-wise. My legs are feelin' the heat."

Bob instinctively looked down and peered at her bare calves; they were cut as a track star would have worked them into shape during that season.

Seeing him enjoying the view, she quickly diverted his attention face-to-face.

"Uh, so you're goin' out of town?"

"Be back next week. Here, on the same day you're going to your interview, to wish you well or a fond farewell.

"Oh, here's the money for the drapes. Keep the change. Gotta go, just thought I'd check in with my peachy partner."

Bob's face flushed as a flashback of that violin fiasco entered his mind. It was sixth grade. After the boys in the class stopped laughing, Janina approached Bob and proclaimed: "That was a peachy performance you just gave. I'm proud of you."

That moment stuck with him all these years. He blushed then, and he was blushing now.

"I'll be here early on the day of your visit. What time are you going?"

"Late in the afternoon. Thanks, I'll need some encouragement."

It seemed to Bob every entrance and exit was a production number for Janina. But it all seemed natural to her. No haughty behavior. Maybe he had misjudged her demeanor. What did she say? She had, through her lifetime, played many charades.

After she left, he sat for an hour or so listening to a CD on the classics. His mind drifted. He thought of Janina as a real classic, a Rolls Royce.

He went off to sleep, snoozing, and awoke two hours later, having slipped off his desk chair face flush with the vent, heat practically burning his face.

So, when will Janina and I share this bottle of wine? It was her favorite. Tonight, for me alone, a salad, some vegetables, no beer after dinner.

It was time to get in shape. Maybe tough times coming. Visit the gym tomorrow. Start a new membership.

Day eighteen for Janina will come next week. Her reputation proceeds her. She was giving this detective thing thirty days. She would be here day eighteen to send me off to my interview. Maybe one last hurrah.

So, this is what it's like to be reborn and start a new career at the age of sixty-plus. Much baggage to cart around.

"Okay, Peachy, we're in this together." He could only hope those were the words she was uttering now.

The eighteenth day would arrive soon enough. Maybe by then, I'll have lost enough weight and size to fit into my old digs.

So, hope springs eternal in the whatever. The eighteenth day can't come soon enough.

DAY 18

The following week drifted by slowly with a few court dates. Why weren't more husbands responsible for their marriage vows? Especially when there were children involved.

Never found any ladies I could get permanently attached to. Never a great shake with any of our town's females. Worked with most of the movers and shakers in the area, but none to wed.

Coffee on. Juan Valdez would be proud. Heat up. Cozy atmosphere.

A knock. Janina entered, her voice somewhat muted. "Had a rough week. Two conferences on ethics and the law at Grand Valley. Maybe a joke for this state. Will present findings to a new state ethics commission.

"Lost at the regionals. Chess matches. Not even an honorable mention. And let's not get into the tussle I had with Father Stan. My music is too avant-garde for his liking. Tone it down for the old-fashioned traditional crowd."

"So, but overall, your week went well. Perhaps somewhat unexpected, however," Bob lamented. Janina plopped down next to Bob.

"This swivel chair needs a cushion. I've got a contact. Down filled. Plush.

"So, you're off this afternoon to your interview with that patriot. Well, pack your heat, dear boy." She looked at Bob and raised her eyebrows.

He thought sympathy, empathy, or just plain pathetic.

"Well, okay, we'll meet in a couple of days. You can debrief me. I'll keep an eye on the actions at the capital. That Emergency

Powers Act goin' for a vote in a few days. Takes effect thirty days after that."

"Would you like a biscotti—lemon flavored?"

"No time. Gotta catch a plane to Austin, Texas. The law firm wants my briefs on what constitutes an ethics violation in eminent domain cases. Good luck, Peachy, and conceal it well."

She took one visual tour of the office and only uttered, "An area rug. Room needs an area rug." Bob only noted. So today, she just sauntered out of the office. No rush. Maybe getting used to this place. Dropping in. Staying a short time. Some greetings exchanged. Then gone.

The drive to the compound seemed brief. Few words were exchanged between the driver, Senator Pankow's bodyguard, and Bob.

The area was fenced in. The driver stated his business and a gate was lifted. The van traveled half a mile or so to a large communal setting comprised of a farmhouse, two barns, a storage shed, and a large silo with much acreage in the back of these buildings.

Bob and the driver were escorted inside the farmhouse to a small study. Highway Joe was seated behind a large mahogany desk. The room was dark. Joe's bodyguard stood ominously at the entrance to the room. Bob's driver seemed to have disappeared to parts unknown.

"So, you're Senator Pankow's left-hand man. Just want to get to know you boys at the state capital. Hope you took no offense gettin' in here. My man got your Glock. Patted ya down comin' in here, this being our abode and all.

"We're not a fortress mentality here. Everything legal. Just preppin'. Armageddon and all. Got underground bunkers. Fully operational. Time is comin'. The Big Bang the other way.

"No origin of anything. Puff. Outta here. Maybe anarchy,

you say. Bad boys armin' up. No, Señor. Just preparing for the inevitable.

"You don't think we don't know what your buddies in the senate are doin'. They're preparing for war, my friend.

"So, what side are you on? You know there are twenty-two other known patriot groups in our great state. We all know each other. Don't necessarily like each other. But all preparing for that day.

"Are we lookin' to overthrow the government? You go back and tell your friend the senator we aren't lookin' for trouble, but if we find it, we know how to handle it.

"Sorry, can't give ya the cooks tour around the compound today. We got our own maneuvers goin' on—simulation exercises. Computer system all up and runnin'.

"You know, we're the biggest patriot outfit in the state. Today we just coordinating with each other . . . makin' our total gathering the biggest in the country.

"But don't fret, son. We ain't got no bone to pick with you, you bein' what they call an underling. We'll meet with the big boys at the capital when we turn up the heat."

All this time, Bob sat quietly peering at this figure—long, scraggly beard, military outfit, toting a gun strapped to his waistband.

A chill ran down Bob's spine. *So, what am I supposed to report on? I'm the first to get in here, I suppose.*

"Just tell Senator Pankow—okay these folks, anarchists, ne'er-do-wells—are planning for Armageddon—whenever, wherever, however that might be . . .

"We'll have my right-hand man escort you outta here back to your van. Suppose your driver sittin' inside twiddling his thumbs."

This Highway Joe character stood a full five feet four. Two front teeth looked like they had some scrolling on them, an odd blackened color anyway.

Bob noticed two furled flags on each side of the desk with

what looked like a black snake with a bear and a devil's face emblazoned on them.

It was then he thought of the term 'nutjob' and knew he needed to backtrack out of there. To think this place, these people were planning who knows what under the not-so-watchful eyes of any branch of the state government or perhaps the federal boys. Or maybe these folks were being watched. Compiling information. Couldn't our boys raid this place—claim they were insurrectionists? Bob just wanted to find the van and be with his bodyguard, who had strangely disappeared during the interview.

The night air was filled with fog, and a mist sprayed Bob. Shots rang out, bullets flying. Were they coming from the compound?

Bob lay in agony after his ankle was hit. His arm went dead, and he passed out. The night air was thicker but not smoke-filled. Mud covered the body. No movement.

More lights went on in the compound. Men came out into the misty, chilled evening air. Who fired the shots? A state of confusion.

Highway Joe burst out onto the pavement of the parking lot, his gun strapped to his side. His bodyguard came out also and scoured the area around the parking lot. There was no sign of the van Bob rode in. Now, the mist changed to heavy rain, and all was quiet except for the chattering of the members of this patriot group.

Highway Joe looked over Bob's body, smirked, and replied, "Poor fool—a setup to be sure." With Highway Joe, it was hard to tell if the smirk was a sign of empathy or just plain disgust. He always hid his facial expression from his enemies. Keep 'em guessin', he would always proclaim—keep the poor fools guessin'.

The emergency area of the hospital was busy this evening—early morning now—with two attempted suicides, stomachs pumped, an opioid overdose, and a death.

There had also been three automobile accidents leaving six victims in various stages of injury—two life-threatening, pressure on the brain, touch and go. A drunk driver was going the wrong way, entering an on-ramp, causing a head-on collision.

Bob was wheeled in for surgery to remove the bullet. He was losing blood, and his vital signs indicated things were not good. His breathing became labored. The bleeding was arrested. His A Fib was giving the surgeons problems. With an irregular heartbeat in the upper chambers, shock had set in.

Now conscious, he was hooked up to a drip and another tube for life support.

"He's choking on his own phlegm, and his gurd condition is backing up," another surgeon noted. "Clear his throat." Another tube was inserted into his mouth down into his throat.

After surgery, he was wheeled into a room where he was sedated and made to rest.

DAYS 19–20–21

Bob was conscious and aware of activity outside his room. A nurse had been in to visit several times.

He was told a bullet had grazed his left arm, tearing pieces of flesh off. He was also struck in the left calf. That bullet was removed.

The police would be in to take a statement. Bob dwelled on what had happened, his mind a jumble of twisted memories, some facts, some his own impression.

A reoccurring thought, however. *Why had I been so negligent—stupid even—to allow myself to be put in such a position?*

So, in fact, I was a pawn. In some world, somewhere sinister people plotted. Maybe to overthrow the state's governmental machinery. Anarchy.

Or maybe those four senators were actually trying to save the state from crumbling into chaos, and I was a small pawn, a monkey in the middle.

After a knock on the door, a face appeared. From a statuesque form, he heard, "How you doin', Peachy?"

Janina filled up the room with her presence. "Don't get up on my account." She pulled a chair over to the bedside. "I see you finally got a room with a view. Nice botanical garden in the courtyard."

"Okay, yeah—I'm the nutcase. It's an adventure I wanted. An adventure I got. Happened so fast. I high-tailed it out of that compound. Then wham, bam, thank you, ma'am."

Bob noticed she placed a bouquet of flowers in a vase by the window. "Nice drapes—expensive. Nice facility, too. Should I ask how you're feelin'?

"I understand they removed a bullet. Got some news. Are you up to it? Police been around yet?"

"Yes, I'm up for your news, and no, they haven't been here yet," said Bob, trying to sit up. "And how did you know what happened? I suppose word gets around fast back at the capital." He slumped back down.

"Did some digging. Got sources. Used my Sassy Lassie ways, putting the muscle on a few of my semi law-abiding posse.

"You know who brought you here. Lookin' out after ya. None other than Highway Joe Smotherman. He actually took a liking to you.

"None of his boys laid a hand on you. The bullets flying came as a shock to Joe.

"I've got my source here in this place says the bullet came from a Glock 22 40 S&W cartridge. Same gun type issued to our legislators' bodyguards. It was your driver who plugged you. Snuck around the back of the compound—made it look like one of Joe's boys hitting you in the back from the compound.

"It was supposed to have done you in. You're one lucky dude," said Janina, smiling, the room lighting up.

"Old Joe went to the press immediately. Quieted the already nervous press and the pals who are keeping their eyes and ears glued to this insurrection business.

"Wonder how your boss, Senator Pankow, feels, having thrown you to the wolves. The wolves threw you back." She looked up at the ceiling. She watched the *drip, drip, drip* of liquid entering Bob's body.

"Yes, you certainly do have a taste for adventure. This is another fine mess. They'll cover it up, the big boys at the capital.

"Now, you still don't know who your secret admirers are payin' you that cash. Getting confusing, isn't it?" Janina came closer to Bob. So, my thirty-day trial period is coming up. So, I'm in deep with you also. Frankly, I didn't want to go this far.

"Now, the whole court system knows I'm tailing your behind. Not quite in bed with your shenanigans, but pretty close.

"I've got eyes and ears everywhere. Lay low, I say. Let the politicians play out their hands.

"You're not fodder yet. Still hanging in there. You're gonna have to wait for your secret admirer. Is he spendin' more cash on his plans—now gone wrong—you not being the collateral damage he hoped for?"

Bob's eyes closed. Sleep was calling. He looked at Janina and made an observation before she left. "Balenciaga—cashmere wool—black and gray logo scarf."

Startled, Janina's mouth turned upward; her brows lit up. Now her teeth shone bright, dimples evident. "Correct—your fashion sense, dear boy, improving immeasurably." She came closer. Bob was now flat on his back. She squeezed his hand and started forward to kiss his cheek but stopped abruptly.

"Business before pleasure. Too much business here to attend to." She left.

Bob would spend another day here. The police questioned him and claimed they would "look into the matter." Bob doubted every word they spoke. *Thank you, Highway Joe Smotherman. You saved my hide.*

DAY 22

The phone rang. The voice was muffled, curt, and threatening. "So, your butt is still intact. You know we are the good guys. So, we noticed no one from the senator's office came to your bedside. And you haven't visited his office since the shooting. Sounds strange, doesn't it?

"We want you to smooth things over with the senator. Find a parcel in his office loaded with marked bills. Go in after hours. Don't care how you do it.

"Bills are marked. We'll trace 'em to an account and prove extortion.

"You got that Sassy Lassie lady to help you. She's been snoopin' around. It's spy versus spy, old man. You are the monkey in the middle again.

"You get the bills. We'll call in forty-eight hours—two days—2 PM phone call.

"State of emergency's been declared. The Fab Four have it wrapped up. On the move. You still livin'. Didn't need your body to stir up animosity against the patriot groups.

"Now, all this patriot business seems like small potatoes to these senators. They're takin' kickbacks every which way.

"They're usin' the Emergency Powers Act to curtail everyday commerce in the state. Not letting certain pharmaceuticals in the state, wreaking havoc with the transportation industry, and choking off the food supply industry. Not letting produce get to the vendors and stores to sell—unless bribed, of course.

"They can, through the act, freeze bank accounts, making big businesses unable to buy and sell in the marketplace.

"These patriot groups are a diversion. Your Highway Joe friend is a decent enough character. Rough around the edges. Former hedge fund trader. A do-gooder himself but caught up in all this Armageddon stuff, world comin' to an end and all.

"Commerce is beginning to slow down now. State departments can't pay their bills, their budgets hacked by these crazy senators. The deep state on their side.

"We know your senator boss keeps those parcels in his personal office safe. Bring it to your office. Forty-eight hours.

"So, monkey man, we'll make it simple for ya. Here's the combination to Senator Pankow's safe: 33 right—28 left—62 right—back 360 degrees left to 62. Open, says me.

"New money is already in your account. We'll tell ya where to bring the bills. Handle with kid gloves. Already in envelopes. Marked. Your friend Pankow; history. He's the bottom of the barrel. The chain moves up from there.

"Maybe you're the catalyst. Blow the big boys outta the water. Maybe you're just another chump wishing things would be normal again. But what is normal, my man?

"Good and evil aren't opposites. One and the same. The swamp still exists. Just different players.

"Find your partner. Much smarter than you'll ever think of being. Knows our dirty turf. Practiced in our field.

"Notice how she outthinks you at every turn. So, you still want this gig. Only my rhetorical reply.

"The only mask you have is in your mind. We set you out there, livin' on a highwire. Like the experience? No one to account for but yourself.

"Some with Sassy Lassie. Her hubby bailin' on her a few years ago. Till death do us part.

"Get your own Glock ready, Mr. Gumshoe. You're in for a bumpy ride!"

And the line went dead.

The door creaked open. "Three-in-one oil will do the trick," said Janina entering, leather handbag in hand, her typical Christian Dior presence.

"You're still intact, Peachy. All limbs present and accounted for."

She slid onto the chair next to Bob. "So, where's my Juan Valdez? Light dairy cream. You're buyin' store-bought half percent milk. Sense of style . . . sense of style.

"London weather. Needed my parapluie today. French for more class than the bumper shoot crowd.

"You've healed somewhat. Just a light cast. You were a target. Went on the hot seat.

"So your plan 'A' went bye-bye. You just following orders. Mr. Anonymous paid you. Don't know if you're comin' or goin'.

"Let's make this an occasion, your survival and all. Then, upon your demise, I could have taken back the drapes, pilfered your excuse for a croissant, and raided your ice box."

Bob, face reddened, "Come on, Janina. Let's get down to your level of business.

"Mr. Anonymous wants to pop Senator Pankow back to the Stone Ages. I—we—gotta get a package of bills—money from the senator's safe, all marked.

"I've been given forty-eight hours. As far as I know, I'm still working for him. After all, they did send me flowers at the hospital.

"We'll go tomorrow evening. I've got paperwork to return to him. Plus, I have a key to his office. Don't know why Mr. Anon gave me the combination to his safe where the money is stashed.

"Easy job. Maybe too easy. But gotta follow orders. More money was placed in my account. Then wait for his call to make a drop."

Bob noticed Janina moving toward the cooler refrigerator. "Pop the cork, Señor. Just a thimble full of drink." She pulled two small demi glasses out of her bag.

"Dooney and Bourke. All leather. Sewn, not glued. Worth

a king's ransom," said Bob, glad to burst forth with this piece of trivia.

"My, you are up on your haute couture. Congrats, Peachy."

Bob's face flushed. Cork removed, they shared a thimble full of wine—Chateau Pichon Longueville Virginia de la Comtesse—Pauillac France—red savory.

"Ah, the French—sophisticated. Delicate. There is no comparison to the gauche English behavior—their wines were dull and stale, and the grapes never fully matured. Even our breed of nasty rain can be redeemed with the French influence.

"Remember to sip, not gulp. So, let's bring back this package and wait for further instructions from your Mr. Anon.

"My sources tell me those four senators have their plan in motion. The Emergency Powers Act sailed through committee now to be voted on. They're already disrupting the economy.

"They'll still go after these patriotic organizations. More like a ruse than anything. Blame them for the chaos about to unfold.

"I canceled two speaking engagements in Texas just to be with you, Peachy and see you through this mess you've created.

"Won't charge you till my thirty-day trial period is up. Comin' on us soon. Keep up on the fashion industry. Mix and match my play always. Maybe someday you and I will make the fashion runways in Paris in the spring. Even there, when it drizzles, it sizzles."

Her exit, again, runway-like. Knob turned. Creaking sound. "Three-in-one oil, Bob. Only hope for this noise to cease."

DAY 23

The usual routine complete, Bob sat and listened to a Three Tenor performance. Nothing on the docket until Janina arrived. Both would make the trek to Senator Pankow's office after hours, open the safe, take the satchel of money out, and bring it back to the office. They would wait for instructions tomorrow at 2:00 PM.

Handle with kid gloves. Bob checked his bank account. More funds. Not quite the amount previous but enough to pay his bills and salt some away. Maybe take a restful trip somewhere warm after this "caper." He laughed to himself when that word popped into his brain—was completed. Just when he didn't know.

This office now felt more like home. Though he knew his home was darker, smelled of stale body and food odors, and was just a one-bedroom apartment in an okay part of town, nothing special.

So, he thought, his whole life—clean living, a career in teaching and law enforcement, a meager pension, some medical coverage. No outstanding debts. Some friendships disappeared as the years wore on. He thought of himself as one of the good guys. Never took a bribe or a kickback; never owed anyone a favor for certain services rendered. Just an average Joe.

He knew the big boys ran every financial show—politics and business—maybe even in the sanctuary, behind the scenes—the spiritual, religious community.

And here he sat with some lady—she Sonic. Her speed seven hundred forty-one miles an hour, always vibrating, screaming to be heard by the human ear, insistent, in charge, racing across time and space but maintaining control, albeit on shaky grounds, he surmised.

Then, he Boom. An explosion produced when a shock wave formed at the nose of an aircraft traveling at supersonic speed reaches the ground.

Two forces crashing at each other. A head-on collision. He, putting up the fences. She, daring him to inhibit her fast-paced sonic behavior. Boom!

The door opened. "You did the trick. Three-in-one oil—congratulations. Everyone at the capital is out drinking and carousing.

"Let's get the satchel of greenbacks. I can schmooze with Mr. Janitor man. He knows more about back-room politicking—who's doing what to whom."

This job was low-key. The money was in the safe. Bob returned some folders—paperwork he had completed. It seemed strange that he was still working for the senator, and no one had followed up on his injuries.

And where was this bodyguard who allegedly shot him? Bullets matching the gun type.

"You'd better secure this satchel. Your little puny three-numbered tin safe here is not safe.

"You know you don't know if Mr. Anonymous had us followed or what kind of nasty games he's playing," said Janina, always the cautious doubting Thomas.

"So take it home. Stay up all night if you have to. I'm comin' with you. Keep us both safe."

Bob frowned. "That's unnecessary. I've got a bigger safe at home. I can handle it."

"No, Sugar, I'm packing some high-powered heat—a derringer on my inner thigh. We need to help each other out here. The other boys comin' with their ammo."

"So now I'm Sugar. First Peachy, now Sugar. All night, we'll both sleep on it and bring the load back here tomorrow." Bob gave in to her commands but saw a bright spot.

"I bought some new upscale croissants. French style. And a Beignet. Put some French jam on a piece. It's to die for."

DAY 24

The call came precisely at 2:00 PM, the voice muffled as usual. "Know you have the satchel. Small bills. All marked. Senator Pankow—toast. His prints are all over the money. Take the satchel to the Allen Street school, in the back. Put the satchel in the dumpster.

"4:00 PM drop today. You will receive further instructions at 2:00 PM tomorrow. Don't tail us. Don't try to outsmart us. You are always in our sights. A success—okay, and another check in your account."

Janina listened on speaker phone. "You do the drop. I'll tail you. Easy peasy. We'll meet back here shortly after 4:00 PM to recap. Your Mr. Anon says further instructions tomorrow at 2:00 PM.

"My sources tell me some thugs the Fab Four are paying are going to pop a few of the leaders of the upper echelon patriot groups—a diversion, to be sure.

"The bribes are rolling in to those senators. Your boss, Pankow, is now squeezed. His butt has been put in a sling with no way out. Jail time.

"Whoever your Mr. Anon is, he's cleaning house one political scabnut at a time."

Bob took a deep breath: "So I'd like to know who all your sources are, Ms. Sonic. You seem to be ahead of whatever curve is out there.

"So, another night of watchful waiting. Can't imagine what happens next. I'm just a courier. Movin' money place to place. Interviewin' possible insurrectionists. Gee, how could I get into trouble for that?"

Janina stood up. Her full six-foot-one-inch frame nose to

nose. Bob recoiled. "You're in this game up to your eyeballs. Everyone's coming for your hide, Mr. Courier. And you don't know the half of it. Just do your job today. I'll cover you with a tail."

"I'm goin' to my retreat tonight. I have other obligations on my calendar. See you tomorrow, Peachy—1 PM. We'll plan more strategy. Keep your eyes and ears on high alert."

"There's more to this intrigue than money. Having problems figuring it all out. Go to the drop now. I'll follow. No need to come back here to recap. Tomorrow at 1 PM then." Janina sauntered to the door and then turned back. "Save the croissants. Day old or not they're better than an English scone any day of the week."

Bob sat for a few minutes. He wanted to time the drop precisely. Janina, he thought, was unusually pensive. Quiet. Mind elsewhere.

The drop was accomplished. In an old neighborhood, the school was a three-story brick building in a poor section of the community with many bungalows and rehab homes around the area.

His mind diverted to his elementary school north of the poverty demarcation line and Janina reciting "Mary Had a Little Lamb" from that makeshift portable stage out to an audience of fellow kindergarten students. It was Bob's turn next to recite "Humpty Dumpty":

"Humpty Dumpty sat on a wall. Humpty Dumpty had a great fall. All the king's horses and all the king's men couldn't put Humpty Dumpty back together again."

The class roared with laughter and jeers, pointing fingers at Bob. His face flushed, and he became embarrassed.

Ms. Stewart told the class to be quiet and calm down. This was a famous nursery rhyme.

She peered at Bob. Damage done. Janina's turn before was greeted with applause. She liked being the center of attention and took a deep bow. If the boys in the class could form a whistle, they would all be puckering up to blow their best tone.

Bob retreated to his seat and became sick to his stomach. Janina continued looking at Bob, her demeanor and expression only known to her—pity, sadness, sympathy, empathy, disdain. Her five-year-old emotions were not fully developed.

At lunch, she offered him her candy bar as a dessert. Bob turned it down and looked away, hoping the day would end and he could just go home. He knew his emotions expressed embarrassment and a bit of self-pity.

How long had this moment from the past lasted? Someone may be watching now.

Get out of here. Go home. A can of what tonight? He was eating healthier and had lost ten pounds since he opened his agency. Overall, his stomach was not churning out of control. Gout controlled. A-fib still with him. Workout regimen working.

Go to the office tomorrow. Janina there. Wait for further instructions. This cat and mouse game had to end soon.

He wanted out. To share the rest of the wine with Janina and move on to the next case. He wanted simpler ones, back to friends of the court. Or simple assault cases. Even a missing persons case or two.

He checked his bank account and saw another amount was put in. Good news.

DAY 25

He tested the door again. Squeak gone. The heat worked. Monthly bills were paid. In business to stay.

Not quite 2 PM. Got up late this morning. Shaved. New style clothing. Chino pants. Slim fit. Flannel shirt. L. L. Bean.

Bob wondered what Janina's style would be today. Books checked out from the library. Fashion design A to Z.

At 2:00 PM, no Janina. No call yet. No panic yet. Maybe this fiasco was over. He had read in the news about a bloodbath. Two of the patriot groups were attacked, but by whom? Rumors were that National Guard troops, off duty, stormed a compound. Three patriots killed up in the UP.

Then, he heard the Teamsters were planning to put more taxes on the double tandem trucks, those weighing more than eighteen thousand pounds entering the state. The four senators were putting the squeeze on the trucking union.

No Janina yet. Bob jumped out of his seat. The phone blared. "Hello." The muffled voice was not so muffled.

"Listen carefully. You did your good deed, Mr. Boy Scout. A clean drop. Events are moving fast. Our boys are pinning Senator Pankow's ears back.

"You're still the monkey in the middle, my friend, but your lady friend is too high profile. You notice she's not with you today. We had to shut down her snooping around. Just temporarily, we hope. She's in a safe place. Not of her own accord, however. So listen carefully. No one's gonna get hurt. Seems Miss Sassy Lassie collected a file full of data and info on the four senators—the kickbacks, bribes, extortions, the whole nine yards. She planned to take them to her judge friend and set up a grand jury. Good intentions but bad judgment on her part.

"Over these past six months, she's been putting together her own case file. We want you to go to a small office she rented across town and pick up the documents. Bring them to 233 Marshall Street, where we first met you.

"She's been using you and your detective agency as a front to bring these senators down. Things got too hot when the senators' boys moved in. Even her muscled associates couldn't protect her."

"You so much as harm a hair on her head—" Bob stopped short and teared up.

The voice continued: "Now, now. We have no beef with the lady. In a way we're protecting her. We got our job to do. She's got hers. And you, my friend, are on our payroll.

"The address is 505 Carey Street. You've got twenty-four hours. You'll be followed. Pack your heat. Wouldn't be surprised if Senator Pankow knows you're workin' for us."

"So help me, she'd better be safe. I want out of your business. What do I care what those senators are all about or who you are and what you're all about?"

"Just bring us those documents. That file. Break in. They're in the tall filing cabinet.

"Maybe the senator is on to you. Good luck. You know we'll put a tail on you. We'll cover you as much as possible but can't guarantee anything.

"She'll be safe as long as all goes well. Don't screw up. The event's comin' to a head."

The phone went dead. Now, his stomach began churning. At first, in anger, then his mind went blank. Bob thought of himself as a giant screwup. A naïve jerk who wanted some change in his life. *So, Janina was playing me. All that nicey, nicey stuff just to use my office and this detective agency as her cover. And now I'm taking the brunt of this whole mess.*

Bob had mixed feelings. *Okay, so I'm beginning to like her. She with her haughty ways. She was mellowing, wasn't she? Giving him credit for trying to understand the cultured fashion world?*

Good wine, good food, high-end designer clothing . . . oh, what the heck. Who am I kidding? I'm just a poor sappy fish out of water. Jeans and an old denim shirt my sense of style.

But I miss her presence. His head was hurting. Another migraine. *Okay, go get the files. Take them to Mr. Anon. Wait for him and his crew to do whatever they must do. Their civic duty.*

Mostly, he longed for Janina. Was she okay? Where was she? Not in hiding on her own accord?

Maybe thirty years ago, I'd play the role of the savior, making everything right, Sir Lancelot charging into danger and saving the queen from an arch enemy.

Today, reality. I'm too tired. My a-fib actin' up, and I'm on blood thinners. So many doctors to report to.

Go to your flat. Open up a can of something. Soup Du Jour. Hit the sack.

Do your duty tomorrow. Take your tools with you. Pack your heat. Take those files to Mr. Anon.

Yeah, okay. Monkey in the middle. Janina, I hope you're safe and sound. Today you didn't get a chance to see me in my chinos and fancy L. L. Bean shirt. Bob fell asleep.

DAY 26

A little cubby hole in the wall was Janina's other office. It was easy to break the lock. The files were in the corner. Bob broke the lock on the cabinet, knowing this was low-grade dirty work.

I don't give a rat's ass if I'm tailed. Anger building. Files in hand. No thugs to beat up. No tails.

Now, I take this polluted folder to Mr. Anon. This routine is getting old and stale. Too many pieces of doo-doo to put together. And of all people to betray me. I tried to change to meet your standards, Ms. Sassy. Cross the t's; dot the i's.

So where do I go? No home. No comfort. Me, just a nice guy. A sucker. One born every minute.

The hooded figure answered his pounding on the door at 233 Marshall Street. A muffled voice said, "Give me that folder."

Bob complied.

"Now leave. Don't look back. Don't ask questions. Back to your office."

"Is Janina okay? Where is she?" His mind said bust this whole operation wide open. His body said I'm worn out. Get me out of this nightmare. Goodbye. Close up shop. This detective racket business stinks. "You bastards better be keeping her safe. So, you outsmarted her this time. Cat and mouse—"

The door slammed shut in his face without mentioning when Mr. Anon would call again or where Janina was being held captive. *But then, wasn't she playing me with all the sweet talk and requests to make the office homey?*

What did she have on the four senators and Senator Pankow? Bob assumed the senator's aides knew what he was doing—

digging up information. But there was nothing here to dig up. Just a courier.

And who was Mr. Anon? Who was he working for or with?

Bob slept in the office that evening. In the morning, he would take the sign down from the door and close this place down. He would go home and just be a senior, attending meetings at the center and going on a few casino trips. Maybe he would take up wood-carving. Most of Bob's golf and school buddies had already gone down this path, the path most traveled.

Gag me with a spoon. So, I feel sorry for myself. Suck it up, buttercup. One of Bob's football coaches pounded in his head from the old days when a steel-toed boot from the coach penetrated his tailbone, and he couldn't sit down for a week.

The new ways. Subtle messages. Weaving and bobbing. The rules bent, reworked, and bent again. No one in charge.

No one telling you the truth you dumb son-of-a-bitch. Didn't your First Lt. dad tell you not to eat crow? He called you a "peck-erhead." Pump that gas at the station. Wear that rubber bow tie. Say yes ma'am and no ma'am. Check the oil, pump that gas. Sell, sell, sell.

He was startled when the phone rang. "You have done well, monkey in the middle. Our efforts have proven successful. Your highwire act is coming to a close.

"Tune in to today's headlines. But this is just the beginning of our draining our great state's swamp. So, you weren't expend-able after all. Darkest before the dawn and all that rotty rot.

"Janina's safe at a safehouse—477 Park Avenue. Pick her up. Word has it you haven't called her JJ since you first met.

"Why so formal over these past few weeks? She'll be there tomorrow. Go to her and report back to your office for a 2 PM phone call." The muffled voice went dead.

Over a can of beef barley soup, a can of beets, and a piece of apple pie purchased that day at his favorite market, Bob focused on the news.

"On the way to a conference on Patriot threats in Grand Rapids, four state senators were struck by an eighteen-wheel semi-Peterbuilt truck. A tragic accident but all survived and are in serious condition with life-threatening injuries. The senators will be confined for weeks at Grand Rapids General Hospital."

"In other legislative news, Senator Dawson Pankow was indicted on bribery and embezzlement charges on the take from the Teamsters union, which also has members under indictment. A federal grand jury will look into this and other charges brought against other legislative members."

DAY 28

The door opened at 477 Park Avenue to a small, dingy room with closed curtains. It was stuffy, and the heat wasn't working.

In a corner was a body strapped to a chair, mouth gagged and duct-taped, rope binding the legs to the chair.

"Crap, JJ," Bob said, slumping to his knees. *Sugar, Peachy . . . tears flowed. Balenciaga. Well-coordinated. Still wearin' my chinos and L. L. Bean flannel shirt.*

Oh, who am I kidding? He removed the rope first. Then the duct tape, knowing he wouldn't get a word in edgewise. So much to discuss—what, where, why, when.

She stood. A full six foot. Still in charge. "So, you are my Lancelot. A literal demotion in the myth business. I'll keep my metaphors straight, however. So, you are my knight in a somewhat dulled tin shield. I'll take that to the bank."

He wanted to hug her. She backed away. Plenty to discuss. Back to the office. Mr. Anon filling us in at 2:00 PM.

"But why the abductions? Who are these people? What do you know JJ?"

"Soon enough, Peachy."

The ride back to the office was subdued. Neither spoke. For Bob the confusion persisted. Should he be angry. Distant. Uncaring. All this was unwinding in a very troubling way.

Janina's demeanor was hard to read. Everything under control. Was this the end of their togetherness? It wasn't a relationship, really—rather some perfunctory game. This JJ is perhaps using Bob, her own motives only known to herself, and maybe also those of her inner circle. But who were they?

The phone rang on time. Again, a muffled voice, though more raspy this time. "So, you have two birds of a feather back together. Hey, a rhyme. Look, kids, you've helped us chase the bad guys—catch 'em and cripple 'em a bit.

"Those senators ran into an eighteen-wheeler. No accident there. And Mr. Pankow got his nads in a vice.

"Bob, we've got your back. Don't worry about Pankow's staff comin' after you.

"And JJ—smart cookie that you are—you got too close to the fire. You may know too much—who we are and who we represent.

"Now you two kiss and make up. Let bygones be bygones. No harm, no foul, and all that kind of stuff.

"One more thing, Bob. Let ya in on a secret. Been meanin' to tell ya my whole life. While your violin playin' in the sixth grade was a bit screechy for my taste, I was the only boy in that class who didn't make fun of you." The phone went dead.

Bob stared in confusion at Janina. Janina stared back with more intensity. No one spoke for an endless two minutes.

Janina spoke first. "Okay, I came here almost a month ago to see what you had going on. I was in deep with the investigation. My contacts gave me enough information to put those goons away for a long time. You were a perfect cover for me. You, a newbie in this detective business. Me, the slick old-timer. Then you, too, got in deep. Maybe you, the naïve courier, carrying out Mr. Anon's orders.

"I went along in my own brazen way, but I got used to your bumbling ways. You have actually made a go of this detective business."

"So, you used me. Shame on me for trusting anything you were doing or your haute couture ways," said Bob with a look of disgust.

"I'm a jeans and flannel shirt kind of guy. Sketchers I can walk into. At my age, I'm having trouble always bending over to tie my shoes. My a-fib is getting worse. My gurd is out of control. My nerves unsteady. My diet improving. Less sodium in the canned Boyardee I'm ingesting. This new job—the career change is taking its toll." His head slumped. He teared up.

"Get a grip, Peachy. Life's too short to have regrets. You'll figure it out and do the right thing eventually. I gotta go. Be back here day after tomorrow. Got VIP business to attend to."

She made her usual departure runway style. She turned and opened her mouth to say goodbye but turned back and quietly closed the door.

DAY 29

Pleasant dreams. Morning at the office. No calls. Quiet. He read a fashion book. He wore jeans, a flannel shirt, and Sketcher shoes with false laces—walk-ins, no ties.

DAY 30

There was a soft knock on the door. She entered. "Our names are still on the door. Me Sonic. You Boom.

"Coffee brewing, I see. Nice croissant. And the label on the jar—Provance Shiek, elegant. Okay, I'll have one of your Pop-Tarts occasionally."

She carried a large case under her arms and placed it on the floor. She popped open the clasps and took out a violin. "Peachy, play for me. It's all tuned up. I borrowed it from one of my orchestra friends who plays in the local symphony. What was that song you played in sixth grade? Reuben, Reuben. Come on now you can get through it. I won't laugh. I'll be too busy singing along. Got the sheet music right here."

Bob blushed. "Can't do it. Forgot everything. How to hold the bow. Where the fingers go. JJ no can do."

"Take the leap of faith. Retrieve it from your memory bank. Breathe slowly and don't panic. Pick up the violin. Under the chin. I've put resin on the bow," said Janina encouragingly, giving Bob the violin and bow.

He tucked the violin under his chin. He remembered the notes A-E-D-G and screeched a few draws. He remembered his teacher said this was a peppery tune. *Play it quickly with conviction*, she would say.

Janina looked at her sheet music. "One, two, three." Both started out of sync. Then, the leap of faith. The tune reverberated throughout the room. The sound bounced off the walls and out into the alley through the open window.

For three minutes, Janina and Bob were a duet. Comfortable.

All in good health. Fun. For Bob, even joyful.

The playing and singing ended. Both parties treating each other. Janina looked at Bob and laughed—not a maligning menacing laugh but a joyful belly cajole.

Bob blushed again and smiled, self-satisfied. So, this is what joy is all about.

Janina came closer to him. She wiped a bit of jam off the corner of his mouth and kissed his cheek. "Business before pleasure. But a little pleasure between the two of us won't hurt anyone.

"Day thirty, Peachy. I've made the decision. You and I are a team. Sonic and Boom. I'm here to stay. In for the long haul."

THE END
(but only the beginning)

Reuben, Reuben

Reuben, Reuben I've been thinking
What a great world this would be
If the boys were all transported
Far across the Northern Sea!

Reuben, Reuben I've been thinking
What a strange world this would be
If the girls were all transported
Far across the Northern Sea!

Reuben, Reuben I've been thinking
What a strange world this would be
If the boys were all transported
Far across the Northern Sea!

Reuben, Reuben I've been thinking
What a weird world this would be
If the girls were all transported
Far across the Northern Sea!

Oh, my goodness gracious, Reuben
What a sad world this would be,
If the boys were all transported
Far across the Northern Sea!

Oh, my goodness gracious, Rachel
What a blue world this would be,
If the girls were all transported
Far across the Northern Sea!

www.ingramcontent.com/pod-product-compliance
Lightning Source LLC
Chambersburg PA
CBHW041607240626

47164CB00009B/203